Off

MARIETTA MIEMIETZ

DEDICATION

To my grandmother, whose brief illness forced me to take time off other endeavors and whose speedy recovery allowed me to fulfill my lifelong dream of writing a book.

CONTENTS

ACKNOWLEDGMENTS

I would like to thank my family and friends for their advice and patience with my distraction while writing this book. Most importantly, I would like to thank my mother for her editorial comments, without which this thriller would probably have remained incomprehensible for anyone who doesn't work in investment banking.

1 PREMONITION

"You don't look happy, darling."

"I'm not feeling happy."

Aline dropped another pair of socks into her bag and stared gloomily at her battered old suitcase as if it were to blame for her woes. Her boyfriend Jim took a more positive view of her upcoming travels and gazed almost wistfully at her partially packed suitcase.

"Come on, it can't be that bad. In fact, I almost wish I could come with you. A romantic stay in a haunted castle down in Cornwall sounds a hell of a lot better than my bank holiday weekend."

"I don't know where you're getting the haunted castle bit from. It's just a dilapidated country cottage that has belonged for generations to a family of noblemen-turned-paupers. And you know you can't come with me because the thought that any AgriBank employees could interact with the outside world scares management out of their wits."

"Plus I have the small matter of a pitch-book to attend to. My boss is meeting a prospective new client next week and I don't want to be to blame if we don't win any business."

Jim sighed. He had been prepared to work long hours when he had accepted a job in the M&A department of one of the most successful global investment banks, but he had secretly hoped for an occasional weekend off.

"You should consider yourself lucky to be working for a bank that actually cares about business. They're getting to be a rare breed. My job seems to be all about internal politics."

"Yeah, I know. You've told me time and again that this famous Head of Research of yours is the first person from his family in three generations who needs to work for a living. So you can't expect him to be very good at it."

"Except he's not called *Head of Research*, but *Super-Sector-Leader*, because after they fired my old boss, they couldn't call his successor *Head of Research* for legal reasons."

"Anyway, I think it's cool. None of my line managers have ever invited me to their family country residence", Jim marveled while watching Aline dump an entire stack of candy bars into her suitcase.

"And besides, I wouldn't put all that chocolate right next to your silk blouses and cashmere sweaters, because it will probably melt. The weatherman says it's going to be the hottest weekend so far this year. Are you really worried that they're not going to feed you at your seminar?".

"As I've explained to you, it's not a seminar. It's a *team-building off-site* and I wouldn't be surprised if making you eat the grub your colleagues had collected for you in the woods was their idea of teamwork. But maybe you're right".

Regretfully, Aline removed the candy from her suitcase. She loved chocolate, but she was even more attached to the garments that were sitting neatly folded at the bottom. She finished packing in silence before curling up on the couch next to Jim.

"I know it sounds like fun. But you have never met any of my colleagues. I'm just not comfortable around them", Aline murmured. She could not begin to fathom just how uncomfortable she would be within seventy-two hours.

2 MOORLAND MANOR

An awkward silence reigned during the long bus ride from London to Sandy Cove in South West Cornwall. Aline's colleagues appeared to be in their usual zombie-like state, which caused her far greater embarrassment on this journey than it did at work. She had grown accustomed to ignoring her surroundings in the office, where she focused on her research and her external contacts. But on board this bus, she did not have a keyboard to play with or a Cisco IP phone to call her clients, and she soon ran out of tasks to perform on her blackberry. Was she expected to engage her co-workers in conversation? Or were they enjoying the last hours of solitude before the round-the-clock display of team spirit that would surely be expected of them once they reached their destination? She briefly considered plopping down next to one of the other analysts and chit-chatting about some irrelevant topic. But she could not think of a good opening line and was put off by the possibility that one of these anemic-looking creatures would just stare back at her helplessly.

Aline wished she could have used the journey time to get caught up on work. Vincent Worthington, recently appointed to the position of Super-Sector-Leader at the Agricultural Bank of Southern England, possessed an unrivalled ability to invent busywork for the department on top of the tasks she needed to perform in order to build her own franchise in the marketplace. As a result, her to-do list had reached epic proportions and she could hardly afford to take the entire bank holiday weekend off. But working on a laptop was out of the question and even reading was risky in light of management's admonitions. Vincent had made it clear before departure that he expected his analysts to take their mind off work and other distractions. He demanded full dedication to this off-site meeting, the purpose of which still eluded her.

The outrageously expensive two-day course in the art of teamwork appeared to be an end in itself. There didn't seem to be any connection with

AgriBank's business or clients, a phenomenon Aline had grown used to in the wake of a major management reshuffle that had taken place six months earlier. The reshuffle itself had been fallout from a series of refinancing operations and strategic reorientations that had been necessitated by the financial crises of 2008 and 2011. Until then, AgriBank had enjoyed an enviable reputation as one of the steadiest and most pleasant employers in the City.

But in 2008, heavy asset write-downs and liquidity fears had prompted the mid-sized bank to take on board two strategic investors who took a more short-term view on its operations. This in itself had proved to be somewhat disruptive to AgriBank's business. Nonetheless, the traditional British lender had managed to muddle along fairly well when the French bank *Credit Continental*, which had taken a sizeable stake in AgriBank as part of the initial recapitalization plan, had to be bailed out by a Russian-Chinese-Brazilian syndicate that had been formed hastily in order to prevent the collapse of this major lender during the 2011 banking crisis. The ensuing boardroom reshuffle had culminated in a patchwork quilt of cultural identities and incongruous business plans that AgriBank employees were now expected to deliver against on a day-to-day basis.

Unsurprisingly, confusion had reigned ever since, and middle management had developed a growing reluctance to take any firm stance with regard to any subject whatsoever. During Vincent's rare speeches to the department, he rarely mentioned clients and did not appear to be concerned with the content of his underlings' analytical work. He merely liked to convey the impression that his research analysts were not doing enough of whatever it was that they were supposed to be doing. In theory, Aline's strong work ethic should have made her a favorite with management, but the harder she worked and the more business she generated, the more disapproval she seemed to meet with. Admittedly, her coverage of the banking sector occasionally comprised pointed remarks about the state of the industry that her own management could have done without, but even her least controversial pieces usually gave rise to poorly concealed displeasure in the upper echelons.

If there was a key to pleasing management, she did not have the faintest notion what it might be. While Vincent's attitude had intrigued and puzzled her, it had never given her cause for concern. She was a rising star among equity analysts, AgriBank provided her with a fairly adequate platform and if she ever found that some moronic management team was not sufficiently supportive of her efforts, a space at a rival firm was bound to open up sooner or later. In short, the world was her oyster.

For the time being, however, she was confined to her seat on the bus her company had chartered to take her to a remote setting for the sole purpose of schmoozing with her co-workers. To her relief, the vehicle was large, with the number of available seats outnumbering the travelers more than twofold. She had been concerned that the group would be as space-constrained on the bus as it was in the office. Instead, she had two seats all to herself, and the two seats across the aisle from her were free as well.

The atmosphere was therefore rather peaceful, and as she looked out of the window and contemplated the scenery, she was only dimly aware of her immediate surroundings. Their journey took them through picturesque villages where time appeared to stand still, dense woods composed of tall, majestic trees that allowed only thin rays of sun to penetrate, salty marshlands and dry heathlands until they finally reached the spectacular, rugged coastlands of Cornwall. They drove past patches of Cornish heath, where delicate, lavender-colored plants that looked even more fragile in the soft evening sun stood solemnly amidst dry grass, as if they took pride in their ability to make do with what they had. The sea, which had taken on a deep blue hue, shimmered invitingly as gentle waves lapped around rocky beaches. This was how Aline had always imagined England based on narrations by Agatha Christie and Arthur Conan Doyle. Sherlock Holmes had travelled these roads over a century ago, followed by Miss Marple and Aline's famous compatriot, Hercule Poirot.

Aline's reveries were interrupted only twice during the long journey. The first interruption occurred when Vincent dutifully sat down next to each one of his charges for approximately two minutes at a time and engaged them in small talk. Aline politely thanked him for his kind invitation. In a grave manner that seemed at odds with the triviality of the occasion, Vincent replied that while team-work was of paramount importance, many people paid insufficient attention to collaboration on a day-to-day basis; hence his decision to hold a team-building off-site. He looked deep into Aline's eyes with a characteristic sad, pleading look on his face before he scurried over to his next underling, just as he did at regular but infrequent intervals at the office.

Vincent had his own office one floor above the research room, where Aline and her colleagues sat packed like sardines. He rarely graced them with his presence, and Aline suspected that his rare visits were sparked by a sense of managerial duty rather than a genuine desire to interact with his staff. As far as Aline could tell, there was not a single research analyst who seemed to entertain cordial relations with him. She did not understand why he appeared to feel so ill at ease among them. True, he had only recently taken over the department in the wake of a management reshuffle which had effectively resulted in his demotion. He was probably aware that his new role was widely viewed as a step back. He had not been involved in a single analyst's hire; every one of Aline's colleagues had been recruited by one of Vincent's many predecessors. This might partly explain his sense of isolation, she mused. But it did not seem to provide a satisfactory explanation for the strange emotion

5

that flickered in his eyes whenever he was face-to-face with Aline – an emotion which she struggled to place and which seemed to bear a resemblance to fear.

One of Aline's colleagues was responsible for the second interruption. Julia, a young oil & gas analyst, chose the precise course of action Aline had briefly contemplated and subsequently rejected. She plopped down on the seat next to Aline and started chattering cheerfully. She nearly succeeded in creating the impression that they were high school students on a field day. Aline could not make Julia out. She seemed normal enough at first glance, but her outgoing personality was so blatantly incongruous with the morgue-like atmosphere at the office as to create a profound impression of disregard for etiquette, in the nature of a guest wearing full evening clothes to a casual get-together. The other analysts seemed to avoid Julia. Aline had been unable to gather the reasons for their distrust from their vague, deprecating statements. Management appeared to harbor similar feelings. Vincent's predecessor, Jonathan, had sought to undermine Julia wherever possible. But Vincent's own behavior was the most striking. Although the working environment could hardly be described as congenial, during his rare visits, Vincent had a strange habit of asking analysts whether they were happy. His tone varied. Depending on the analyst, he would put the question jokingly, hesitantly or in a paternal manner. Whenever he asked Aline if she was happy, his voice had an odd, pleading quality, as if he were afraid that she would answer in the negative and leave him to deal with some unknown consequences. He never put the question to Julia. Whenever he stood next to her desk, Julia would look up at him with a cheerful, mischievous grin, and he would stare at her in blank terror, to all appearances unwilling or unable to utter a single word.

From the first day, Julia appeared to have taken a liking to Aline. To the superficial observer, there was no reason why the two girls shouldn't be friends. In fact, they had a lot in common. Both were recent arrivals; Julia had started her job with AgriBank a mere two months before Aline had joined. Both had moved to London from the Continent; Julia had grown up in Germany, while most of Aline's childhood and adolescence had been spent in Belgium. They were driven and took pride in their work; on most evenings, they turned out the lights at the office. Julia seemed to be generating research and unearthing new clients at a mind-boggling pace and frequently offered to introduce Aline to her contacts. Julia's friendship would have been the perfect cure to the feeling of loneliness and hopelessness that assailed Aline every time she set foot in the dismal office - if Aline had been able to feel at ease in Julia's presence. She was not sure why Julia made her nervous. Was she simply afraid that her unpopular colleague would further alienate her from her other co-workers, thus adding to her isolation while her career prospects at AgriBank diminished? Or was there something else, something in Julia's demeanor that filled her with a vague sense of apprehension?

6

While Aline was pondering the question, Julia carried on chatting excitedly.

"You know what happened at that residence, right?" she asked, undeterred by Aline's apparent lack of interest.

"I don't, and I have a feeling I don't want to know."

"Well, I think sooner or later you're going to hear about the tragedy that took place there. It explains a lot."

"Whatever."

"I know what you mean, but I think it would be prudent not to say *whatever* in front of Vincent. He was badly shaken by it all. Anyway, let's see how this weekend goes."

Aline's curiosity was aroused in the manner in which a reader's curiosity might be piqued by the back cover of a book. If she had been reading a mystery novel, she would have flipped to the part that described the tragedy that had struck at Moorland Manor. But in real life, she felt a strange reluctance to embroil herself in Vincent's family affairs. There was something unreal about this little, hunched man with the sad eyes, and Aline intended to keep it that way. She felt no desire for any aspect of her office-life to become real. She possessed a remarkable ability to concentrate on her work. Whenever she immersed herself in her projects, the lifeless AgriBank employees, the menacing tone of any communication by management, Vincent's incoherent speeches, the strange silence on the over-crowded research floor, the cheap plastic desks and the dirty old carpets tended to fade into the background, like an ugly piece of faded tapestry in a furnished room. She preferred them to remain in the background. Any attempt to inquire into their motives or motivations was bound to let them take center stage – a development Aline was determined to avoid.

To her surprise, they did not stop at a restaurant for dinner during the long journey. She was even more baffled by the absence of complaints about this omission. Admittedly, her colleagues seemed unfazed day in and day out by the abysmal working conditions that ranged from freezing temperatures or a complete breakdown of the air-conditioning to the department's television set running at maximum volume levels while Aline was desperately trying to make herself understood on the phone. But surely they ate dinner? Or had they possibly stepped right out of some *Twilight* saga, waiting to feed on human flesh and blood after dusk? Aline shook her head in disbelief. She could only hope that somehow, there would be some food waiting for them upon arrival.

The sun was setting when the bus drew up in front of Moorland Manor, near Sandy Cove. The rambling old country mansion rose majestic and stark against the darkening sky. Built over a hundred years ago on a grass-topped cliff, the grim three-story stone building overlooked the sea. The water lay eerily still on this calm summer evening. The setting was vaguely reminiscent of a haunted castle, Aline thought. Jim would have been delighted. The bus driver turned off the engines and Vincent took the microphone.

"Welcome to Moorland Manor!" he announced in the proud tone of a host greeting his guests. Apparently, he was deeply attached to his family property, irrespective of any tragedies that might have occurred there. "As you know, the bank has very generously paid for this trip, and my family is making this residence available so that all of you can get to know one another better, far away from the distractions of the office. To keep you focused, I ask that you hand your blackberries, mobile phones, i-pads and other electronic devices over to me. I will return them on the way back to London. While I collect your phones, I will hand each of you a sheet of paper with the name of your room written on it. You have twenty minutes to unpack, and then we will all meet again in the drawing room to discuss dinner."

Aline was indignant. The audacity of asking her for her personal phone! She had previously lamented her management's socialist mind-set; they had always seemed to attribute little value to personal development objectives or satisfaction in the work place. Now, things were taking a decidedly Orwellian turn. At least the prospect of having her own room lifted her spirits. She was not sure what sort of accommodation she had expected, but in light of the open-plan office space, where nearly forty people were crammed into one room, she had come prepared to spend her nights in an outsized dormitory. She remembered that at the start of her first semester at university, her room had not been ready on time and faculty staff had tried to coax her into spending the first to weeks at a youth hostel, sharing a dormitory with thirty other students. "It'll be a lot of fun!" they had promised with a glitter in their eyes that had made Aline shudder. She had preferred to start the semester late and miss a few lectures, but clearly, turning around on her heels would not have been an option on Moorland Manor.

Relieved at the prospect of privacy, at least during whatever short hours she would be allowed to spend in her room, she reflected on Vincent's cryptic remarks about the evening meal. How could you discuss dinner? In her book, you either ate dinner, or you skipped it. There was nothing to discuss, unless the weekend's team-building exercises entailed the joint drafting of a gourmet critique column. Maybe Vincent had meant to say that they would choose a restaurant in the vicinity together. If so, Aline hoped that Italian, her favorite, would win out. In any case, she kept her fingers crossed that there would not be much of a lobby for Japanese food, as she did not share the world's apparent enthusiasm for sushi. Would she have a veto right in the event of a sushi motion? If so, would a veto place her firmly in the non-team-player camp, making this weekend even more of an ordeal than it already was? Chances were that all of these considerations would be a moot issue, since she strongly suspected that there were not many restaurants in the vicinity to choose from. In fact, Aline doubted that there were any shops or theaters or neighbors within a radius of twenty miles. The desolate manor was by far and away the most isolated piece of land she had ever visited.

Vincent interrupted her train of thought, handing her a note with the name of her room scrawled across it. She would be staying in *Dartmoor*. What sort of a family invented names like this for rooms in a private house? In Aline's opinion, hotel or office meeting rooms named after famous cities were already painful enough. She preferred not to probe into the mind-set of people who named bedrooms in their own homes after cities that were best-known for their penitentiaries. Vincent looked at her expectantly and she obediently handed over her company-provided blackberry.

"I think you also have a mobile phone", he said, with just a hint of menace in his voice.

Aline briefly debated how to handle the situation. Of course, she could deny that she had brought a personal mobile phone, but she suspected that Vincent had seen her holding her little orange device in her hands during the journey. In any case, her assertions that she did not possess a personal phone would sound implausible. She felt indignation rise again. She did not see any reason why she should tell a lie. After all, there were no rules against the use of personal mobile phones outside of office hours!

"I won't use it during the seminar", she replied with finality, hoping that Vincent's upbringing in a family of blue blood, albeit limited means, would prevent him from discussing the matter further. But she had underestimated his obstinacy. He shook his head sadly and held out a hand. Loath to make a scene, she reluctantly handed over the offending phone, hoping that she had either deleted all the texts in which she had complained bitterly about the working environment at AgriBank, or that Vincent wouldn't bother to read them.

Twenty-five minutes later, Aline was standing in a large, old-fashioned kitchen, absorbed in the mundane task of slicing pickles. The 'discussion' about dinner had consisted of assigning chores to each analyst. Julia was busy setting the table, while several other analysts were preparing food. Aline mused that she should have predicted that her stingy company would never foot the bill for a restaurant dinner or caterer. Chances were that the bus ride alone had pushed them well over budget, and that management would soon embark on a frantic cost-cutting drive, indiscriminately slashing business travel, taxi rides and market data subscriptions. At least, the pantry at Moorland Manor was well-stocked. There were shelves carrying loads of potatoes, tomatoes and carrots, every variety of tinned food imaginable and a large refrigerator that contained cheese, ham and dozens of fresh eggs. Aline, who shunned domestic chores whenever possible, had to admit that this old mansion, which she had so scornfully referred to as a dilapidated country cottage, was surprisingly well-tended. Except for Aline, everyone seemed to be enjoying their household duties. The crowd in the kitchen was slightly more animated than she had ever seen them at the office.

"Hey guys, I found some fresh mushrooms!" Fred Frobisher, the food retail analyst, cried excitedly. Aline had always thought it fitting that he should cover the food sector. From his simian face to his hunched back and ape-like way of speaking, everything about him created the impression that peeling bananas was just about the most difficult task he was capable of performing. "That will be a nice finishing touch for the salad."

Aline opened her mouth to announce that she hated mushrooms and would much prefer for them to be served on a separate plate, but thought better of it. Loudly refusing to eat something your colleagues had prepared for you during a team-building weekend was probably tantamount to carrying a sign that read 'I am a maverick'. It would be far more prudent to pick out the mushrooms from her salad during dinner, in the hope that her fellow travelers would be too polite to comment on the mushroom pile left on her plate. Next to Aline, Roger, one of the capital goods analysts, was cutting tomatoes into minute pieces, as if he were trying to invent a new nanomaterial, and a tall auburn-haired researcher who had arrived recently and never been introduced to Aline asked no one in particular if they had any idea how much milk you needed to make scrambled eggs. Vincent only intervened once, when Tom Kearney, a conceited young banks analyst who had joined Aline's team several months ago, tried to open a bottle of vintage *Baron de Rothschild* he had found in the wine cellar. Aline's boss did not seem to notice or care that one of his underlings had opened a jar of expensive caviar.

After the welcome distraction of preparing food, they sat down to dinner in an almost Gothic atmosphere. The lamps on the walls gave only a dim light, and so they had lit candles that flickered every time someone passed the butter or reached for the water decanter, throwing grotesque shadows on the walls. They were nibbling their food in silence and, in Aline's case, hiding a growing mushroom pile underneath a piece of half-eaten bread, when Vincent, somewhat belated, tapped his glass with a spoon. Thirty-two pairs of eyes turned to him obediently. Aline hoped that he would be brief. Over the years, she had developed the ability to look sufficiently interested and appropriately amused during boring speeches, but Vincent's ramblings were usually pitiful to the point of causing his listeners embarrassment. His welcome speech was no exception; Aline cringed at his pathetic attempts at burlesque.

"I am happy to welcome you to Moorland Manor", he began with an air of grandeur. "But I have no illusions. Most of you are not thrilled to be here. You are probably asking yourself *Why am I spending my bank holiday weekend in the middle of nowhere?*" Vincent let his gaze wander around the room until his eyes rested on Aline as if he had witnessed the scene with Jim on the eve of departure. "You are wondering *Is this guy nuts to charter a bus and invite his whole department to stay at his family's property?* He will need to up his insurance premium! ". He gave a hollow laugh at his own joke. It was a bizarre habit of his; he frequently giggled stupidly after announcing bad news. At times, Aline doubted his sanity. "But make no mistake, you will get to a point in your career when you will be grateful to me. The world has changed. The competitive landscape for Research has changed. You can only succeed as a team. If you don't work together as a team, our long-term competitiveness is at stake. So far this year, this department has produced only three joint pieces of research. I'll be frank: that is not enough. The good news is that you still have four months to turn this around."

I'll be frank was one of Vincent's favorite lines, and he generally used it whenever he seemed to be at his most hypocritical. Aline felt resentment rising within her once more. She was all for collaborating with her co-workers whenever they had a common goal. However, most of her analyst colleagues covered different sectors and wrote for different audiences. There was simply no overlap between their research reports, and she had wasted many valuable hours trying to find enough common ground to warrant the production of one of these joint pieces that seemed to be *en vogue* at AgriBank.

"If you say to yourself *I'm a good analyst, I know my sector, clients rate me and therefore I will get a good bonus,* you are wrong!" Vincent continued. To Aline's surprise, anger sparked his voice. "And the repercussions won't be limited to your bonus. If you don't turn this situation around, then I can't guarantee that you will have a job next year!" He pronounced these last words with fake regret and just a trace of menace in his voice, but switched to soothing paternal tones as he continued. "I know it's not easy for you. Teamwork is still not taught sufficiently at school and university. That's why I have brought you here. In unfamiliar surroundings, far away from any distractions, you will perform team-building exercises. You will learn to trust your colleagues. And in doing so, you may save your bonus – and your job. Enjoy your dinner." He nodded at his underlings with a quiet air of satisfaction and sat down.

If his speech had crept out Aline's colleagues in the same manner in which it had affected her, they betrayed no sign of it. Everyone around her was eating calmly, with their usual expressions of boredom and detachment stamped on their faces. Aline went over Vincent's speech in her mind. None of it had rung true. She was fairly certain that someone else at AgriBank had lent his voice to Vincent, who as far as she could tell did not have any opinions of his own. Maybe this was why no one came close to him; his robotic qualities made it impossible to get a message through to him. *But who had effectively ghost-written these lines for Vincent and why? Could you learn to trust your colleagues, just as you learnt to use a new piece of computer software?* she wondered. She didn't understand why things had to be so complicated. Surely, people were capable of sitting down together and just getting on with their work where necessary, without spending a weekend involved in bizarre games? And why did Vincent have to remove them from their familiar surroundings, as he had put it, in order to imbue them with a sense of team spirit? The more she thought about it, the more she disliked the strange emphasis he had put on the words *unfamiliar surroundings*. So absorbed was she in her thoughts that she did not notice the furtive glances Vincent darted at her as she sat across from him, mechanically removing mushrooms from her salad.

The beauty of travelling with listless people was that nobody suggested any after-dinner activities. Aline escaped to *Dartmoor* at the earliest opportunity, which presented itself shortly after eleven pm. She had to admit that apart from the macabre name and possible link with family tragedies, the room was not bad. It was spacious and the furniture and hard-wood floors, while showing signs of wear and tear, had clearly been expensive, as had the faded flowery tapestry on the walls. Most importantly, the king-sized bed had been fitted with a fairly soft, thick mattress. The only real drawback was that the door wouldn't close completely. Aline tried several times to move the doorknob so as to allow the lock to snap in, but her efforts were in vain. It was obviously broken, and she eventually decided to leave the door ajar. Sprawled on the big, comfortable bed, the world looked much brighter. Mechanically, she reached for her phone to text Jim, but felt nothing but empty space. Puzzled, she groped around in her bag. The phone wasn't there. In a flash, she remembered that it had been confiscated for the duration of the weekend. It didn't matter; she knew he wouldn't worry as he clearly thought that she was in good company, surrounded by hard-working and infinitely boring investment bankers. Exhausted, she turned the lights out and went to bed.

She had been drifting off to sleep when she suddenly became aware of another presence in her room. She did not have time to react. She heard soft steps approaching rapidly and felt a weight on her left leg. When she looked up, she found herself gazing straight into a pair of yellow fluorescent eyes.

3 NOCTURNAL ADVENTURE

"Well hello there", Aline murmured tenderly and held out a hand. The little black cat that had just jumped onto her bed sniffed it curiously. It was still young and frisky; it pawed at a strand of Aline's hair that fell forward as she bent down to caress the animal. The kitten rubbed its head against her hand, then fell down on its back and purred. Several minutes later, it jumped to its feet and left as rapidly as it had arrived. Another twenty minutes later, Aline was sound asleep.

It was still dark outside when she awoke to the sound of a moan. She checked her watch. It was not even five am. What was that sound? She listened attentively. There it was again, longer and with greater intensity than the last time. There was no doubt about it, someone was in agony.

Hurriedly, she put on a long cardigan and stepped into the aisle. The moan was coming from a shared bathroom at the end of the corridor. When she opened the bathroom door, an arresting sight awaited her. Roger was hunched by the toilet, his hands pressed to his stomach, his face contorted.

"Are you okay? Is there anything I can do?" Aline asked, genuinely concerned.

Instead of a response, Roger vomited copiously. Aline was at a loss what to do next. Under normal circumstances, she would have called an ambulance. But *The Powers That Be* had confiscated her mobile phone, and she doubted that she would be able to locate any ambulances waiting close by in the event that a mystery illness should break out on Moorland Manor. Chances were that by the time an ambulance arrived, Roger would either have made a full recovery, or would be too far gone to save. Was there a medicine cabinet in the building? And what drugs were you supposed to administer to a patient with severe gastrointestinal symptoms of unclear etiology? While she was pondering the question, the door flew open and Tom rushed in. Seeing that the toilet was occupied, he dashed straight to the sink and emptied his stomach contents into it. When the turmoil in the bathroom subsided, Aline could distinctly hear someone else moaning in one of the bedrooms. Before she could reflect on the strange coincidence that all of her colleagues should become ill simultaneously during a company off-site held in a secluded spot, Julia stepped into the room. The look on her face held both surprise and alarm.

"What's going on?" she wanted to know. "Is this some kind of a new summer vomiting bug going around?"
Like Aline, she seemed unaffected by the mystery illness.

"I have no idea what this is all about or what I'm supposed to do." Aline shrugged helplessly.

"Not much we can do, to be honest. Maybe check everyone's pulse and temperature and clean up the mess in the corridors."

Aline closed her eyes and shuddered. She had secretly hoped that all those who had been taken ill had made it to a bathroom on time and was distressed by Julia's revelation that this was not the case. The two girls set out to work in silence, in turn taking each colleague's wrist, then holding a hand to their foreheads. No one seemed to be about to faint or to be running a high fever. They checked every room on their own floor and the floor above, until every analyst was accounted for. Everyone was ill, without exception, some experiencing a moderate level of discomfort, while others were visibly in agony. When the girls reached the conclusion that they had done all they could for their unfortunate co-workers, they cleaned up as necessary and returned to their rooms.

Aline checked her watch. It was shortly after six am. She would try to sleep for a couple more hours, she decided. For a few minutes, she lay still, anxiously monitoring herself for any signs of the outbreak. Was she experiencing the first symptoms, very faintly, of nausea? *Stop imagining things and go to sleep,* she scolded herself. She counted a mild form of hypochondria among her principal weaknesses and knew that she would be able to diagnose the symptoms of just about any illness in herself if she listened to her body long enough. Exhausted, she finally fell asleep.

4 BETWEEN A TREE AND A HARD PLACE

Breakfast on Saturday morning was a cheerless affair. Nobody was eating, either because they were still feeling ill, or because they did not trust the food following the night's events. Even Vincent was running late, on the grounds that he had passed a very bad night. Since he slept in a different wing of the building, Julia and Aline had not seen him when they had nursed their colleagues. Looking ashen, he asked feebly whether anyone else had been ill. Most of those present just confirmed by nodding their heads. Only Tom added belligerently: "Seems everyone was ill – except for Aline and Julia." Aline felt thirty-two pairs of eyes boring into her like daggers.

Health issues notwithstanding, the group soon proceeded to the first team-building exercise on the agenda. Standing outside in the blazing sun, Vincent outlined how they would build mutual trust by climbing trees together.

"Once you have trusted your colleagues with your life, you will know that you can trust them in business", he declared importantly.

Trust your colleagues with your life? Aline had come prepared for some mildly embarrassing interactions with her co-workers. She had not expected to find extreme sports on the agenda. And Vincent's logic was completely flawed in her mind. *Surely no one wanted to be served with a lawsuit for dropping an opponent from a tree top,* Aline thought, but did not verbalize, *but office politics were a different matter altogether.* She had no inkling how soon she would have to reconsider the theory that no one on Moorland Manor wanted to hurt her physically.

Vincent divided them into groups. Aline was assigned to climb a tree together with Tom, Fred, Amanda and Julia. This play of chance – if it *was* a play of chance – came close to a disaster scenario. These four were the colleagues she would never have chosen for any endeavor whatsoever, least of all for any activities where she risked life and limb. In her mind, Tom was a lazy and utterly useless young whippersnapper, who tried to hide his inferiority complex behind a breath-taking self-righteousness. Aline, upright and independent of character, was always put off by his hallmark *holier-than-thou* speeches and was regularly at a loss how to deal with his unpredictable passive-aggressive behavior. As an absolute beginner who had recently entered the complex world of equity research, he naturally struggled to produce meaningful reports and to gain recognition in the marketplace. Aline blamed management, who expected anyone with basic reading, writing and googling skills to morph into a fully-fledged analyst overnight, instead of allowing young professionals to grow into the analyst role over time by supporting senior colleagues. But for some inscrutable reason, Tom had always blamed Aline for his inadequacy as an analyst, nurturing jealousy that bordered on hatred. On his first day in the office, he had arrived with a friendly smile on his pudgy little face. The smile had soon given rise to a perennial sulk that verged on the comical.

His best and seemingly only friend Fred complemented his passive resistance very nicely through a highly active display of aggression. While Fred never seemed to utter a word on the research floor – Aline even doubted that he ever spoke to any clients – she had often overheard him dripping poison into someone's ear by the coffee machine. That someone all too frequently was Tom, who seemed to have an overwhelming desire to hear that the world was unfair and that he was being subjected to some nameless injustice.

Amanda was even more annoying than the two guys, if that was possible. While Fred and Tom confined themselves to philosophizing as an outlet for their self-righteousness, Amanda engaged in one charitable activity after another in an effort to save the world in the most conspicuous manner imaginable. Worse yet, she documented her progress very avidly and very publicly. Aline shuddered as she recalled Amanda's recent participation in an AgriBank-sponsored marathon to support some *Corporate Citizen* charity. Amanda had provided e-mail updates about her training on an almost daily basis via the centralized distribution list, sharing pointless and frequently unpalatable episodes with the entire department. Her detailed account had covered the electrolyte imbalances she had suffered as a result of her physical exhaustion at a level of granularity that had far exceeded the boundaries of good taste.

And then there was the inscrutable Julia. While Aline did not have any specific reproaches, she had decided that Julia appeared too normal to be real. Everything about her was business-like, friendly, practical and resolute. She never complained or moralized. Instead, she quietly got on with her work, superbly ignoring management's extravaganza in the process. No one else at AgriBank seemed that normal. *It had to be a façade,* Aline mused, *like the perfect maid in an Agatha Christie mystery that invariably turned out to be a crook or thief on a grand scale.* Aline had yet to form a theory as to what exactly Julia might be trying to hide behind her innocent façade.

Not only was Aline stuck with her least favorite colleagues on this August Saturday morning that would have been so perfect for a long stroll along the Thames with Jim, but the instructions for the tree-climbing-trust-building exercise that Vincent was reading out aloud were simply abominable. When he had concluded, each group set out to discuss the configuration that would get as many group members as far up the tree as possible, as this was the criterion to be used by Vincent later to declare a winner among the six teams. In Aline's view, which she wisely kept to herself, this athletic competition seemed to be more apt to put peer pressure on non-tree-climbers than it was to build trust.

"I suppose we can consider ourselves lucky", Julia announced with a smug grin that appeared to be laced with a slightly diabolical quality, "to count the lightest, most athletic analyst, who is not afraid of heights either, among our group."

All eyes turned to Aline, who was kicking herself for having revealed details about her trapeze class to her colleagues. During a conference dinner several months ago, she had racked her brains for a non-work-related and non-contentious topic of conversation, in a desperate attempt to build something resembling a rapport with other members of her department. Her trapeze class had been the first thing to come to her mind, and so she had blabbed her secret to a bunch of couch potatoes who had clearly never been face to face with so exotic a creature as a hobby trapeze artist. She had only herself to blame if she was now being selected as a guinea pig for this demented and undoubtedly dangerous exercise.

The tree that had been allocated to Aline's group looked particularly worrisome. Even the lowest branches were so high up that the analysts needed to form a human ladder to reach them. Fortunately, that part of the exercise passed uneventfully. As the tallest member of the group, Fred lent support to everyone else as they attempted to access the tree. Subsequently, the others pulled him up in a joint effort. Climbing further up the tree presented greater difficulties. The sparse branches were spaced relatively far apart and were getting disconcertingly thin near the tree top. After some deliberation, it was decided that Julia and Amanda would stay in the lower part of the tree, while the men, being taller, would have an easier time climbing higher, using the sparse, but relatively strong branches as support. Julia suggested that Aline should subsequently climb all the way to the tree top, on the grounds that she was by far the lightest among the five involuntary athletes, with help from the men, who would by then be securely installed in their respective positions in the upper half of the tree. As she watched everyone climb to their designated positions, showing clear signs of strain in the process, Aline brushed away the suspicion that another reason for selecting her for the most dangerous part of the exercise was the limited value her colleagues placed on her health and well-being.

Finally, it was Aline's turn. She reached Fred relatively easily, but was far too short to transition to the higher branches where Tom was located. There was only one way to get to the tree top. She had to place her feet in Fred's hands, and Fred had to subsequently raise his arms high above his head, while holding on to the tree by means of his knees. With a slight push, Fred would be able to throw her in Tom's direction. Tom, who was also anchored to the tree exclusively through his feet and knees, would hold out his hands to catch her. It was a risky operation to say the least, and in sharp contrast to the training conditions in her trapeze class, Moorland Manor was not equipped with any safety nets. Fred quivered in a thoroughly disconcerting fashion as Aline, the involuntary acrobat, climbed onto his shoulders, but was remarkably steady when she placed her feet on his hands and he raised her high above his head.

"You got her?" Tom shouted to Fred.

"Yeah, sure. She's such a light weight for me, I could hold her in one hand", Fred bragged, his gasps belying his statement.

Aline, who felt that her situation was already precarious enough, was not in the mood for silly jokes. "I'd rather you held on with both hands", she grumbled. Speaking in mid-air, where no one was likely to hear her, was a mistake she frequently made in her trapeze class, and which she was to regret on this occasion.

"What did you say?" Tom asked, bending forward and shifting the position of his outstretched hands slightly in the process, just as Fred pushed Aline towards him. She missed Tom's hands, and for a fraction of a second, hung suspended in space, the ground coming fast towards her face. At the last second, with a presence of mind that Aline had never thought possible in her simian food retail colleague, Fred managed to grab her feet, nearly tumbling out of the tree himself as he did so. Aline ended up hanging from Fred's grip with her head down, slightly resembling a bungee jumper.

She groped for the lower tree branches and as soon as she had gripped one of them firmly and tested its strength, she called out "Thanks, Fred, you can let go of my feet now."

"Are you sure?" Fred asked. "I can pull you up again very easily", he offered helpfully, "that way you won't need to start again at the bottom."
"Sure I'm sure", Aline barked, exasperated. "I am done climbing trees for today."

The truth was that she had only one desire: to plant her feet firmly on the ground again. She was through with climbing trees for the remainder of her stay at Moorland Manor, and possibly for life. She knew that by making her way down now, she was bound to be branded as a party pooper who spoilt the fun for the other members of her group. Her team had come breathtakingly close to victory in the very first team-building exercise, with Aline flying within several feet of the tree top at one point. Now, they were bound to finish in last position, with their trapeze artist unable to claim any firm final position in the tree. Annoyed glances notwithstanding, Aline was of the definitive opinion that her health and, most importantly, her survival had to come first as she scrambled to her feet.

5 HATE MAIL

Aline and her colleagues were allowed to take a short break before the start of the afternoon session, and Aline dragged herself gratefully and somewhat wearily to her room. She had barely touched her lunch, partly because she still distrusted the food that was served on Moorland Manor, and partly because she was still shaken by her flighty tree adventure in the morning. Starving, she reached into her suitcase for a candy bar. It was empty. Cursing, she recalled removing the chocolate at Jim's insistence that the weekend would be smoldering with heat (he had been correct on that count) and based on his assertions that AgriBank would feed her properly (here, he had been wrong!). Why hadn't she at least taken some cereal bars or dry crackers that were less prone to melting in the heat?

She was feeling weak from hunger when she made her way into the library, where the next team-building exercise was scheduled to take place. The library looked very old and ostentatious. The floor-to-ceiling bookshelves were filled to the brim with old-fashioned, used-looking tomes. The extensive ornamentation and the total silence that reigned as a result of the thick carpets and heavy, dusty curtains inspired awe to the point of suffocating anyone who entered this room. Aline was immediately overcome by pangs of longing for the outside world with its blazing sun, colorful flowers and chirping birds. What plans did Vincent have for his underlings in this mausoleum?

To her relief, her line manager asked them to take their seats. At least she did not have to risk depleting her reserves completely with any more running, jumping or climbing. It did not take her long to realize, however, that it was out of the frying pan and into the fire for the AgriBank Research Department. After jeopardizing his staff's health in the morning, Vincent now went on a rampage to bruise their egos. To all appearances, they could do nothing right in his eyes.

"I'll be honest with you", he took his usual opening line. "Our results in the last client surveys were crap." He paused for effect, provocatively looking from one analyst to another.

Julia latched onto his remark. "I thought we were going to prioritize revenues over surveys, at least until the Client Services Department was fully up and running and able to poll our clients properly?" she asked, frowning. She was right. Aline distinctly remembered Vincent's recent presentation to this effect, as well as her incredulity at her employer's dysfunctional internal processes. How could they ever have relied on client surveys as a proxy for commissions and as a tool to assess the research department if they were unable to conduct these surveys in the first place?

Vincent stared at Julia with a puzzled look on his face, as a director might look at an actress who did not stick to the script. Clearly, he had not expected any push-back. There was no good response to Julia's query, and after some deliberation, he pretended not to have heard her interjection. He opted to address it implicitly in his next statement instead.

"I can ask any senior client whether they rate any of you and the answer will be *No*. You are barely ever on the phone to clients. You don't harvest synergies with your colleagues. How many of you have done a joint piece with another research group? In fact, you don't look good on any metric I can choose." He glanced triumphantly around the room. Julia was quiet; apparently, she had given up after this latest piece of twisted, irrefutable logic. Even Aline's natural rebelliousness had been quenched by her Super-Sector-Leader's apparent desire to find fault with everything his staff did or omitted. She could not help the impression that his speech consisted of borrowed lines, that he was a stooge for someone higher up within AgriBank and that resistance was therefore futile. If only she could play fly on the wall in AgriBank's boardroom to get a clearer idea of the name of the game!

After some more ranting and raving, Vincent seemed to decide that his underlings had been sufficiently humbled and proceeded with the agenda by writing the word *teamwork* across a huge sheet of paper that had been fastened clumsily to a bookcase.

"So, what does teamwork mean to you? Aline." He gestured in her direction to indicate that it was her turn to speak.

After her tree climbing ordeal, Aline was not feeling sufficiently charitable to provide the type of flowery answer Vincent was looking for.

"Well", she began with just a touch of sarcasm in her voice. "It seems to be composed of two words: *team* and *work*. I think the two are inextricably linked. So teamwork is really only possible if everyone is willing to work and is working more or less in the same line of business. For example, introducing a colleague from another sector to a joint client could be far more valuable than writing a forced joint piece for an audience that doesn't exist, or risking life and limb climbing trees together. And let's not forget, if everyone does their own work well, that tends to generate revenues, which maximizes the probability that your colleagues will still have a job next year."

Vincent was obviously tired of arguing. He refrained from noting down any part of Aline's reply on his makeshift giant notepad and merely raised his eyebrows in response to her belligerent and borderline hostile statement, before signaling to Tom that it was his turn to have a go at defining the core of that magical conception, teamwork. Tom was exceptionally well-versed in the art of corporate psycho-babble and relished the opportunity to launch into one of his rambling moralizing speeches, especially after his nemesis Aline had provided him with ample scope to improve upon her response.

"To me, teamwork is all about collaboration, trust and mutual respect", he began with his characteristic haughty air of pomposity and self-righteousness that never failed to raise Aline's hackles. "A good friend of mine from university had the immense pleasure of meeting one of the most inspiring business leaders of our time. He described the great man as *simply a good guy.*"

How on earth did Tom come up with the script for his never-ending waffle? Aline wondered. Did modern universities nowadays teach a course entitled *The Loser's guide to getting on everyone's nerves until they leave you alone?* She considered herself to be highly creative, but she could never have come up with anything so elaborately pat and meaningless.

Meanwhile, Tom rambled on, undeterred by the glances of boredom, surprise and annoyance that various of his co-workers darted at him. "In fact, most truly senior figures – CEOs, CFOs, highly placed politicians – are very human, very pleasant to be around."

Aline suppressed a desire to gag and zoned out. While Tom continued his seemingly never-ending pseudo-inspirational speech, she mapped out her upcoming research report in her mind. It was entitled *Chain Reaction* and examined in minute detail the repercussions that the bankruptcy of any one major lender would have on the banking system as a whole. Her aim had been to conscientiously analyze contagion risk on a bank-by-bank basis. She had started the report a few weeks back and had been very excited about the topic until her initial research had revealed that under most scenarios, her own employer would default on its obligations, rendering her deferred compensation worthless in the process. This finding had caused her enthusiasm for her project to wane somewhat, and she had decided to put it aside for a while and to turn to cheerier subjects in the interim.

After some more pronouncements on the nature of teamwork that would have provided sufficient material for an entire army of psychoanalysts, Vincent proposed another game. It was called *Reality Check* and sought to enhance each analyst's self-awareness by comparing their self-assessment with their colleagues' views.

"Here's how it works. You write a note to a colleague, telling him or her how you perceive them. You can sign your name or leave it, as you prefer. You fold the piece of paper, write the recipient's name on it and place it into a bag I will circulate in due course. You repeat this exercise for as many colleagues as you wish. I will play postman and deliver each letter to its addressee. You get a few minutes to think about the messages you received, and then you tell the audience how the message compares to your self-assessment and how it is impacting you", Vincent explained. "Any questions?"

There were none. Vincent distributed notepads and almost everyone began scribbling. Aline was the sole exception: she stared at the white sheet of paper in front of her as if she expected words to magically appear on it. She had steadfastly refused to participate in any note-passing games in elementary school, at a time when writing notes to your friends every time the teacher turned his or her back had been all the rage, and she could not think of any messages to convey to her colleagues now. There was no point in telling anyone that they were the most uninspiring group of people she had ever met, and she was not even sufficiently interested in any of her colleagues to seize this brilliant opportunity to taunt them. Suddenly, she noticed that her inactivity was attracting unwelcome attention. Hurriedly, she bent over her notepad and scribbled *I have nothing to say whatsoever*, folded the sheet, wrote *To no one in particular* in the address section and covered the writing with her hands until she had an opportunity to drop the note into the bag.

Vincent sorted the 'mail' pedantically as his department looked on. He seemed to be under the impression that suspense was mounting as a result of his deliberately slow movements. It took him a long time to distribute the mail, and Aline was bored out of her skull by the time he gave permission to open and read the letters. Aline had received two comments. She immediately recognized the spidery scrawl on the first note: it was unmistakably Julia's. She unfolded the sheet of paper. It read "Hi Aline, you're the only normal person in this room. Let's catch up over coffee when we're back in the city. Take care, Julia." Aline did not have the faintest notion whose hand had penned the second note, which did not bear a signature. It read "You are arrogant, abusive and malicious. If you think you can play cat and mouse with me, you'll soon find out which one of us is the cat and which one is the mouse."

In the sequel, Aline was vaguely aware of Vincent gesturing to Amanda, who seized the opportunity to express profound gratitude for this eye-opening team-building game. While Miss Virtuous waffled on, Aline sat dazed, trying to pinpoint the author of the *hate mail* she had received. Little wonder the document had not been signed. Even her most hypocritical colleagues could not possibly be deluded enough to pretend that this rancorous note constituted well-meant advice from one caring team member to another. And what had driven Julia to pen the particular note she had written? Was she up to something sinister and trying to deceive her perceptive colleague by means of an elaborate show of friendship? Aline breathed a sigh of relief when the coffee break rolled round before it was her turn to take a stance with respect to the messages she had received. She was at a loss as to how she could possibly comment on either note.

When they returned to the library after the coffee break, Julia's seat remained empty. At first, Aline was relieved to find that someone else was deflecting attention away from her own chronic tardiness. However, after twenty minutes had elapsed with no sign of the oil & gas analyst, she began to worry. Eventually, she mustered the courage to ask:

"Does anyone know where Julia is?"

The room fell silent, as it always did whenever someone asked a question in Vincent's presence. Aline had always been intrigued by this phenomenon. Possibly, it was attributable to Vincent's violent outbursts in response to questions that sounded harmless and genuine to Aline's ears. Funnily enough, it was usually Julia who asked the questions that triggered these reactions. Similarly, Aline's query seemed to rub him up the wrong way. He directed a cold, hard gaze at her.

"It's not something you need to worry about", he replied icily. His tone made it clear that he considered the matter closed.

Aline's heart began to pound. She had been harboring suspicions that Julia might be up to something sinister. But following Vincent's curt reply, she grew alarmed that to the contrary, something sinister might have happened to Julia. To Aline's delight, the discussion soon moved on from *Reality Check* to vague observations about the general nature of trust and respect. For the remainder of the afternoon, Vincent rambled on about team spirit and joint efforts and collaborative work in the context of the five-year plan for his research department. Aline's colleagues watched him, their bodies motionless, their faces expressionless. Aline found it difficult to concentrate on his monologue as her mind kept wandering to Julia. As much as she tried to convince herself that the resolute German girl was capable of looking after herself under virtually any circumstances, Vincent's frosty "hands-off" response to her innocent query with respect to Julia's whereabouts kept sending quivers down her spine.

After a while, she could no longer restrain herself. She had to find out. As she got up and made her way to the door, Vincent darted an inquisitive glance at her, but made no effort to try and stop her. Aline stepped outside and sat down on one of the little stone walls lining part of the premises to determine the best course of action. The brilliant sunshine was dazzling, and the heat made everything seem unreal. The stuffy library where her colleagues were being lectured seemed far away now. She looked back at the rambling mansion. In the abnormal brightness of this sizzling hot summer day, it seemed to lie unnaturally still and to grow darker and gloomier by comparison. It filled Aline with foreboding. How many hiding places did this imposing edifice contain? Was Julia hidden somewhere in the house? Or had she already been moved off the premises in a cloak-and-dagger operation?

Aline shook her head impatiently, as if to clear her mind of these dark thoughts. She would have to rely on her wits if she wanted to help Julia. She decided to start her search in her colleague's room. With luck, she would discover that Julia merely suffered from a nasty headache and had decided to take a nap. She knew instinctively that this explanation, though plausible, was not the right one. The feasibility of her plan was further hampered by the fact that she did not know who had been assigned to which room. Therefore, the only thing to do was to check every single room in the South Wing, where the analysts had been accommodated. Her search did nothing to raise her esteem for her colleagues. She came across more pornographic magazines and self-help books of the most pathetic type than she had ever dreamt possible. It was one thing to purchase such items with a view to stashing them away at home and reading them surreptitiously in the privacy of your own bedroom, but who would take them along to a company off-site? While her search was thus revealing in some ways, it did not yield the result she had hoped for. There was no trace of Julia anywhere in the South wing.

Aline went back to her own room and sat down on her bed to think. What next? Methodically, she proceeded to inspect the East wing. She was in for a shock. The grimy walls had obviously not been redecorated in decades. In most of the rooms, the sparse furniture was broken and worm-eaten. Numerous planks in the hard wood floor were splintered to the point of representing a safety hazard. In one of the rooms, she even found a large hole in the ground. A shadow dashed past her and disappeared through the hole; she was fairly certain that it had been a rat. She was beginning to gauge the full extent of the Worthingtons' poverty, and she also understood why her entire department was staying in the South wing. But while her discoveries might contribute to raising her social awareness, they did not bring her any closer to her goal of locating Julia.

She entered the West wing with a growing sense of futility. Perhaps she ought to give up and return to the library, where her colleagues were probably wondering what she was up to. Maybe even Julia had re-joined the group by now. Possibly, she had just tried to profit from the coffee break to run a quick errand and something had delayed her return. Aline realized that she was trying to convince herself of some fabricated tale with a *happy-ever-after* ending because that was what she wanted to believe. She knew perfectly well that there was no errand Julia could possibly be running in this deserted spot.

She was torn from her reveries by a familiar sound, which she could not quite place – a faint click or tap. She held her breath and listened, waiting for the sound to recur. There was nothing but silence. After a while, the silence and the darkness of the hallway became unbearable. Had she only imagined the clicking noise? If not, what could it possibly be? And then the sound recurred with a vengeance. This time around, it was not a single, timid click. It was a furious avalanche of clicks, somewhat reminiscent of a woodpecker pecking at a tree. Only, it was coming from the inside of the building. Aline was sure of it. No outside sound could have penetrated the thick stone walls with such intensity.

There it was again. This time, the clicks came more slowly and sounded less aggressive than before. They appeared to emanate from one of the rooms near the end of the long hallway. Aline took several steps in that direction. The volume of the clicking noise rose with each step, supporting her theory. As she advanced, she became increasingly convinced that the sound originated from the corner room at the end of the West wing. She tiptoed to the door to the room in question and listened. There was no shadow of a doubt now. The clicking noise, which was alternately coming in furious cascades and ebbing away, came from inside the room. With her heart in her mouth, she knocked on the door. "Hello?" she croaked, startled to realize that a croak was all she was capable of. She had intended for her voice to sound firm and steady. There was no reply. With a trembling hand, Aline pushed down the doorknob. The room was unlocked. She pushed the door open and entered.

6 A GRUESOME FIND

"Here you are!" Aline exclaimed. Her voice held relief as well as disbelief. Julia was sitting behind a majestic mahogany desk near a window in the sun-flooded corner room, busily typing away on a laptop. She had obviously not heard Aline approaching. Puzzled, she looked up.

"Any problems?" she asked. "Is Vincent looking for me?"

"Are you alright?" Aline stammered unnecessarily, instead of a response.

"Yeah, I'm fine. I just needed to find a quiet spot to write my company report because it has to go to print in time for the road-show we just won last week", Julia explained apologetically while checking her watch. "Geez, it's getting late!" she added. "We'd better head back or there will be no dinner left by the time we get there."

As they walked back across the long hallway and down a winding staircase, Aline felt decidedly foolish. But her embarrassment soon gave way to frustration and a curious sense of malaise. If it was that simple, if Vincent had merely given Julia permission to skip one of the sessions in order to get some urgent work done, then why couldn't he just say so in response to Aline's question? To all appearances, Julia was safe and sound. But even so, Aline continued to feel ill at ease. She had never considered herself impressionable until she had set foot in this dismal mansion and had been mesmerized by its ominous atmosphere. That evening, she lay awake for hours, mulling the strange events that had taken place on Moorland Manor. It was after three am when she finally drifted off to a troubled sleep.

On Sunday morning, Aline awoke with a start. She had to blink in the sunlight streaming through her South-East-facing window. Her watch read eight-fifteen, implying that she had slept in. She was not a morning person and had not brought an alarm-clock, as she had planned to use the alarm integrated into her mobile phone or blackberry. Now, she knew that she had to hurry if she did not want to be late for breakfast, which had been scheduled for eight-thirty am.

She swung her legs over the side of her bed, jumped to her feet – and let out an involuntary cry. She had put her left foot into something wet and wobbly. To her dismay, she realized that she had stepped onto the remains of a mouse that had been deposited by her bedside during the night. She was positive that the mouse had not been there when she had turned out the light the previous night. The animal was pathetically disfigured. Aline was unsure as to how much of the damage was attributable to a savage killer and to what extent she herself had contributed by inadvertently stomping on it. She felt a cold fury rising up inside her. She did not approve of pranks, and she had no sympathy whatsoever for anyone who deliberately harmed an animal. She vowed to find the culprit and to take him or her to account for this childish act.

Hurriedly, she disposed of the mouse, cleaned her foot, washed her face and carelessly threw on some clothes. When she joined her colleagues for breakfast in the dining hall, she was running only several minutes late. On her way down, she had decided not to mention the dead mouse for the time being. At the breakfast table, conversation remained sluggish. If any of her colleagues had found a dead mouse or any other unpleasant surprise by their bedside, they did not let on. Aline furtively glanced around the room, in the hope that the culprit might betray himself. She could not discern anything out of the ordinary. Yet, the prankster must be seated at the table; no one was absent. The words from the anonymous letter she had received the previous day came back to her: *You will soon learn which one of us is the mouse.* What else did this sociopath have up his sleeve? Would he strike again before departure the following day? *Only twenty-four more hours,* she tried to console herself. As soon as she boarded the bus that would take her back to London on Monday morning, she would be safe. Until then, it was simply a matter of being watchful. Aline reached for her coffee cup. While she was still wary of the food at Moorland Manor, she had satisfied herself that the coffee and sugar could be trusted. As she sipped the sweet, black, caffeinated drink, she felt her spirits return.

By the time she had finished her third cup, she felt ready to deal with anything Vincent might throw at her. She was all the more pleasantly surprised to find that he had not envisaged any formal team-working exercises in the morning. Instead, Aline and her colleagues were left to apply their newly acquired co-operation skills to real life by exploring the environment together, unsupervised, while Vincent busied himself with preparations for the afternoon sessions. As always, a small group had to stay at home to prepare lunch. Amanda volunteered, and two other analysts whom

Aline knew only superficially were ordered to assist. Everyone else made treks towards the beach, only too glad to escape the suffocating atmosphere on Moorland Manor for a few hours. The day promised to be even hotter than the previous day, and Aline was grateful for the sea-breeze as they descended the steep footpath to the rocky beach below. She deliberately took it slow and ensured that she was the last person to make her way down the cliffs. Following her adventure in the tree, and in light of the unexpected present she had found in the morning, she refused to take a chance on one of her co-workers slipping and tumbling down on her.

Her mind was soon taken off spooky events by the pristine beauty around her. From the delicate flowers that adorned the cliff-tops to the massive, rugged rocks that cut mercilessly through narrow stretches of sand, the landscape gave the impression that man had never set foot in this cove. Aline felt herself relax as she watched soft Atlantic waves breaking gently on the shore. Occasionally, seabirds flew past high above her head. If only she could savor this spectacle of nature with Jim, without having to worry about accidents or unspoken threats!

"How are you today?" a familiar voice asked by her side.

She whirled around. Julia was standing next to her. All of the others appeared to have vanished into thin air. She must have spent more time contemplating the scenery than she had realized. Hopefully this excursion was not part of a test to see how long you could tolerate your colleagues' presence! But why had Julia waited here for her, instead of moving on with the others? It had been a deliberate move on Julia's part; this much Aline was sure of. Was her oil & gas colleague simply keen to chat to the only normal individual in the department, as she had put it? Or did she have an ulterior motive?

"I hope you've recovered from your fall in the tree. I didn't realize how hard it would be for you to get to the tree top, or I wouldn't have suggested it", Julia continued in a conversational tone.

"I didn't either", Aline murmured absent-mindedly.

"What do you suppose our friend Amanda is going to *cook up* while she's holding down the fort back at base?"

"Probably nothing much", Aline expressed her wishful thinking. "I think she is just staying home because she thinks fixing lunch for us selfish explorers gives her yet another claim to martyrdom."

"Or maybe after the disastrous charity marathon, she has finally been forced to admit to herself that she's just not athletic enough to take walks along beaches and climb over rocks", Julia suggested with a catty grin.

"Maybe. Whatever she is up to, I'm not eating any food that is served on Moorland Manor!"

Julia frowned. "Aren't you exaggerating a bit? I think you were right to avoid the local mushrooms, of course. I did, too. Sometimes it can be really hard to tell the difference between the edible and the poisonous species, so it's not too surprising that nearly everyone ended up with food-poisoning..."

"You think it was the mushrooms?" Aline interrupted, staring at Julia wide-eyed.

"Yes, of course. What else could it possibly be? Salad vegetables rarely cause any outbreaks."

"But who do you think put the mushrooms in the pantry?"

"I suppose the people who live here", Julia replied, shrugging. "They probably enjoy picking mushrooms when they go hiking in the nearby woods. They were probably going to check out the dubious ones in a guidebook later. My family used to do that when I was a kid in Germany. I don't think the Moorland Manor residents quite realized that a bunch of big city kids was going to take over their house for the weekend and pinch their mushrooms in the process."

"The people who live here?" Aline echoed incredulously. It had not occurred to her that the AgriBank staff might not be alone on the premises. She had not come across anyone during her search of the building the previous day, but then she hadn't checked out any of the rooms in the West win except for the one Julia had chosen to write her research report.

"Yes, of course", Julia replied with an amused smile. "Vincent's family goes back a long way in this region. Moorland Manor used to be the family estate. Now they've largely run out of money and are struggling to maintain the building. But some of Vincent's distant relatives are still living here. I think they use only part of the house, though. You didn't think that this residence was being used exclusively as a venue for corporate off-site meetings, did you?" she added after a quick glance at Aline's puzzled face.
Naturally, Julia was right. Aline had somehow supposed that the place was uninhabited, but of course, no one could afford to leave such a large property empty for extended periods of time.

"How is your room, by the way?" Julia wanted to know.

"Pretty big and comfortable, actually. I'm in *Dartmoor*. Whereabouts are you?"

"In *Broadmoor*. I can think of cheerier names for bedrooms, but the room itself is fairly pleasant. This must have been a fabulous mansion before the family fell on hard luck."

"What exactly happened?" inquired Aline, who had no idea how or why Vincent's family had become impoverished.

"I'm not sure how they lost their money, to be honest. But they're definitely hard up, and of course Vincent never lived down the suicide and his divorce."

Aline felt the same revulsion that had come over her on the bus, when Julia had mentioned a tragedy in Vincent's family. She decided once more that she would not pry into the Worthingtons' family affairs.

"I just hope the place isn't haunted, with Worthington ghosts floating around rattling chains after midnight?" Aline asked jokingly in an effort to steer the conversation back to a more superficial chat.

"Not that I'm aware. I suppose the memories are still haunting Vincent, but as far as nocturnal visitors go, the only one I've had was a very frisky black kitten when we first got here."

Aline had completely forgotten the cat. She hadn't seen it since her first evening on Moorland Manor, and apparently, neither had Julia. Was the cat alright? Would the sociopath who had killed the mouse to terrorize Aline hurt the cat?

The two girls walked on in silence. The light sea-breeze was getting stronger. Occasionally, gusts of wind blew unpleasantly. The sky had been a radiant light blue when they had left in the morning. Now, clouds that were undeniably tinged grey were gathering on the horizon.

"Looks like rain", Aline observed.

"More like a storm. There's actually been a weather warning for the region. I checked it out on the internet yesterday."

"By the way, I asked Vincent where you were and he basically told me it was none of my business. Why all the secrecy, if all you were doing was writing a report on a laptop and checking out the weather forecast in the process?"

"That's Vincent for you. He actually gave me a pretty hard time before he finally signed off on me taking a break to get some work done. He seems to equate a few hours' absence from his team working seminar with high treason. Eventually, I convinced him that we couldn't afford to lose the road-show because my report wasn't ready and he reluctantly agreed. I actually think he's been scared of me ever since I caught him covering up a major glitch, and he didn't want any confrontation. Even so, I had to promise not to tell anyone that I had special permission to miss a session, because he was concerned that suddenly everyone would go off and do their own thing. But I suppose I didn't miss anything, did I?"

"Not if you ask me. But then, you're talking to someone who could have done without this entire off-site meeting."

"Tell me about it. I could have written my report on my roof terrace at home and re-potted my plants. I don't even know when I'll get around to it now. September through November is the main marketing season and then the holiday celebrations start. Instead, I'm dawdling along at some pointless seminar with a bunch of psychos! That *Reality Check* game yesterday took the biscuit!"

"Did you get any particularly nasty messages?" Aline asked casually.

"As you would expect. Allegedly, I'm not willing to share my stocks and my clients, that sort of thing. As if anyone on my team would ever muster the motivation to write about my stocks or call my clients if I transferred them over! How about you? Did your rabid puppy dog Tom send you death threats?"

"What makes you think that?" Aline asked suspiciously.

"I watched him. He was giving you the evil eye while penning his letter." Was Tom the author of the hate mail? Aline pondered this new theory. She knew that Tom felt that he was in her shadow, but did he really suffer from a sufficiently severe form of persecution mania to imagine that she was playing with him like a cat with a mouse?

"What do you think is his problem?" Aline decided to take the initiative and try to glean as many insights as possible from the omniscient Julia. It was uncanny how the oil & gas analyst, shunned by everyone at AgriBank, managed to be in the know with respect to just about everyone and everything that was somehow connected to an AgriBank employee.

But apparently, Julia had not psychoanalyzed Tom in much detail. "I think he just has a massive inferiority complex", she responded, shrugging. "Half the people at AgriBank have an ego the size of Texas and a brain the size of a garden pea. You can't expect it to end well."

The combined effect of the cold wind and Julia's remark made Aline shiver. What exactly had Julia meant by *It won't end well?* Was she merely expecting AgriBank's Equity Research department to lose market share as a result of the low quality research she expected her dim colleagues to produce? Or was she bracing for a personal tragedy?

"Fred is quite a character", Aline pursued nonchalantly. This was as good an opportunity as she would ever get to probe into the complex landscape of the human element at work.

"Yeah, he's your typical primitive social climber, stuck somewhere in between fighting the establishment and trying to milk it. His smear campaigns by the coffee machine are legendary!"

"I know, I've witnessed quite a few of them myself. I'll never understand why Vincent doesn't put an end to his disruptive behavior."

"Oh, but it all works in Vincent's favor. He encourages Fred to antagonize everyone against everyone else because so long as all the analysts are at one another's throats, they're too busy to waste any thoughts on how hopelessly inadequate he is as Head of Research, and his position is safe. I can't say that I blame him, given the turnover at AgriBank. And none of his predecessors lasted very long."

"That makes sense. But I don't see how he benefits from Amanda putting more energy into her charity work than into her job these days. Who needs a Head of Research if his underlings aren't even writing any research?"

"Amanda is a special case", Julia agreed. "She should have joined a soup kitchen rather than a bank."

"Maybe that's why she's staying home to fix lunch – preparation for a new career", Aline chuckled.

"Speaking of lunch, I'm getting hungry."

"And I'm freezing. The weather is starting to turn nasty. Let's go back"

They walked back to Moorland Manor side by side. Aline took precautions to ensure that Julia would not slip behind her at any point, but Julia did not make any move to attempt anything funny. Was it possible after all that Julia was simply what she was trying to be – a perfectly normal and friendly colleague?

7 TRAPPED

Upon her return to Moorland Manor, Aline was so hungry that she even considered eating the food which the stay-at-home group had prepared. Julia's explanation for the mysterious food-poisoning during the first night had seemed plausible and was further corroborated by the fact that Julia seemed to be eating normally. If Julia had any concerns about any foods other than mushrooms, she hid them well. Still, a sense of vague apprehension remained with Aline. What if the omniscient Julia had overlooked a vital fact in her assessment of the situation at Moorland Manor? What if Julia was behind some or all of the mysterious events after all? Aline could have chalked the food poisoning up to a series of mishaps, if it had not strangely coincided with her narrowly avoided accident, the *hate mail* she had received and the dead mouse. She decided not to take any chances and spent most of the lunch hour sipping sugary tea, reasoning that it would elevate her blood sugar level sufficiently to get through another dull afternoon of fake teamwork-related discussions. And within twenty-four hours, she would be on her way home!

She was in for an unwelcome surprise. Vincent had apparently grown weary of preaching to deaf ears in his library-turned-classroom and had prepared another practical exercise. It involved a sadistic variation of the popular hide-and-seek game and was even less to Aline's liking than the previous morning's adventure in the trees. Vincent divided the department into two groups. Each individual from the first group, which Aline had been assigned to, would be blindfolded and taken to a secret hiding place by someone from the second group. To this end, Vincent had written the name of each prisoner-to-be on a separate piece of paper. He had subsequently folded all the paper scraps and placed them in a bag. One by one, the captors drew the names of their prisoners from the hat.

Vincent drew first. To Aline's horror, her name was written on the scrap of paper he pulled from the bag. Was it just her imagination or was he looking at her smugly as he made the announcement? When all the names had been drawn, the captors proceeded to blindfold their respective prisoners. They were then asked to leave the room one by one to find a hiding place for their charges and to subsequently return to the library. Once all the prisoners had been tucked away, the captors would start searching for them, with the obvious exception of the individual they had hidden themselves. The idea was that by relying on your colleagues to rescue you from captivity, you learnt to trust them.

Vincent marched off first with Aline. Whatever hiding place he had chosen for her, he was taking her to it in the most roundabout way imaginable. They walked up and down numerous flights of stairs and took more turns than Aline had thought possible in this rectangular house that had seemed composed predominantly of long straight corridors when she had been looking for Julia a day earlier. Her sense of direction had never been very good, and she was soon lost. She had tried in vain to peer through the dark cloth in front of her eyes; it had been securely fastened around her nose so as to shut out every single ray of light. The sense of foreboding that had taken hold of her as soon as she had set foot inside Moorland Manor came back stronger than ever. *Maybe it would be best to bolt and to escape here and now,* she thought, but Vincent's tight grip and the blindfold rendered the idea impractical. With the faculty of sight taken away, her attention was focused on the ominous sound of the rising storm outside. At home, she loved snuggling up on her couch while thunder rolled and rain battered against her window-panes, but the gale-force winds that were blowing across the wide open space surrounding Moorland Manor sounded downright menacing. Aline shuddered. *At this time of day tomorrow, I will be on the bus that will take me back to London,* she tried to console herself once again.

Finally, they arrived at Aline's designated hiding place. She was made to sit down on a cold, tiled floor; then, she heard a door being shut right next to her. To her alarm, she heard a key being turned in the lock. Shortly thereafter, she heard a second door being closed and locked with a key, this time more faintly. A cold terror came over her as she realized the full scale of her predicament. As far as she could tell, Vincent had taken her to a room behind another room and had locked both rooms with a key! Would the colleagues that came looking for her be given keys to all the rooms? Would the idea even occur to them that Aline had not just been hidden, but actually locked away? Would anyone hear her if she screamed? A desolate sense of isolation came over her. If only she was still in possession of her mobile phone! The fact that it had been taken from her upon arrival under a flimsy pretext now appeared in a new and sinister light.

Her anguish conspired with the effects of forty hours of starvation. Suddenly, she felt very weak and on the verge of tears. Her hands shook as she reached for the knot of her blindfold. She did not manage to untie it. She broke out in a sweat and realized that she needed to take a break. As she lay down on the cold, hard tiles, she began to panic. How long until someone found her? Was she even meant to be found? What would Jim and her family think if she simply disappeared during this team-building off-site? Would they drive down to Cornwall to look for her, or would they simply accept her disappearance as fate? Would they ever suspect that any AgriBankers attending the team-working off-site might be involved in her disappearance? She found it hard to believe that life had brought her to this. After all, she was Aline Alexandre, daughter of an eminent physicist and a successful TV presenter. It seemed as if she had accepted her dream job with AgriBank only yesterday. It was perplexing how fast her life had unraveled. Her dream job had soon turned out to be a poisoned chalice. And now, hunger, sleep deprivation and fear had depleted her reserves. She was feeling light-headed. She told herself that she must stay conscious and awake and think, but the thoughts kept slipping from her mind before she had a chance to reach any conclusions or map out a course of action. An obnoxious noise filled her ears. When it subsided, there was nothing but a deafening silence; her blood pressure had plummeted.

When she had recovered her senses, she decided that it was time to take a good look around the place she had been brought to. This time she succeeded in removing her blindfold, although it took her a while - partly because the knot at the back of her head had been tied tightly and expertly, and partly because her fingers were shaking nervously. She was less and less convinced that she was participating in a simple team-building exercise that formed an integral part of standard corporate folly. She had always sensed that Vincent disliked her and felt ill at ease in her presence. What if there was more to it? What if he was genuinely afraid of her for some demented reason that she would never be able to guess? She did not remember having said or done anything that could in any way compromise Vincent's standing with the firm, but she had often suspected that he was not always completely rational. It would not be altogether surprising if he turned out to be a cold-blooded murderer. Chances were that he had deliberately taken her to this locked room on his family estate so as to move her out of the way, either temporarily or – she swallowed hard – permanently. She tried to recall the first phase of the name drawing. Vincent had handled the bag and the paper before anyone else had touched them. He could easily have worked it so as to draw Aline's name without arousing suspicion.

The more Aline thought about it, the more she became convinced that she had to escape – fast. With a tuck, she pulled the loosened blindfold away from her eyes. With the exception of a thin ray of natural light on the floor, the room remained dark. Aline had been locked in a windowless room, but the faint light informed her that the door led to a room fitted with windows. While the thought was somewhat reassuring – at least she knew that she had not been taken to a system of subterranean dungeons – it did not suggest any specific course of action. The fact of the matter was that for now, she was trapped in near-complete darkness, unable to make out the shapes or colors of any objects around her. Systematically, Aline began to touch every item. The room was small, and most of the contraptions she came across were made of ceramic. Fastened to one of the walls was a rectangular object with a glass front that could be opened by pulling knobs. It contained shelves and an assortment of bottles and tubes. There was no doubt about it. She was locked in a windowless bathroom that probably served as an en-suite to one of the master bedrooms. There was only one escape route: through the door which Vincent had locked. He had left the key in the lock. Would she be able to get hold of the key? For the first time, she regretted not having been a girl scout as a kid. For all her academic prowess and ability to build strong client relationships, she was hopelessly inept when it came to survival skills.

She had to give it a try. It was her only hope. She had to find a device that was small enough to push through the lock and cause the key to fall down close to the door, and then to find a way to retrieve the key. It was easier said than done. She examined the objects in the bathroom cupboard one by one, but most of them were flagrantly unsuited to her purpose. People tended to stock bathroom shelves with beauty aids, rather than toolkits that might come in handy for people who were trying to open locked doors. After fingering a seemingly endless row of shower gels and body lotions, she finally discovered a manicure set. *The nail file or scissors might work,* she thought. Grimly, she set to work. It was not an easy task, but the key moved eventually. With a thud, it fell down to the floor, closer to the door than Aline had dared to hope for. Using the nail file, she moved the key towards the edge of the door. The combination of her delicate fingers and the imperfect fitting of the doors in this old house, which left a relatively large crack between the door and the floor, enabled her to pull the key into the bathroom. She breathed a sigh of relief as she unlocked the door and stepped into the adjacent room.

As she had surmised, she found herself in a bedroom. It was a large room that contained a bookshelf, a table, two chairs and a walk-in closet, in addition to a king-sized poster-bed and a small bedside table. And it was clearly in use. A half-empty teacup was sitting on the table, a pair of slippers had been pushed underneath the bed, and a pajama had been draped over a chair. Outside, rain was beating furiously against the window-panes and the sky had grown dark, but she did not dare to switch on the light. Aline's mind was made up to flee from Moorland Manor as soon as humanly possible, even at the risk of being labeled a rugged individualist for life and never receiving another call from a head-hunter again. But as she gazed out of one of the windows that was rattling in the storm, it dawned on her that an escape via that route was not presently feasible. She was on the third floor and the gutter would be difficult to reach even in dry weather conditions. Even if she made it to the ground safely, she might have to walk through the rain for hours before arriving at the next village. And she had no idea where the next village was located.

It was preferable to repeat her trick to get hold of the key and to sneak through the house in an effort to reunite with her colleagues. Once she reached them, she would be safe. Whatever Vincent's plans, he would not dare to do her any harm in front of more than two dozen witnesses. She smiled bitterly as she reflected that in some ways, Vincent's prediction had come true: for the first time since joining AgriBank, she had to rely on her colleagues, trusting them in a matter of life or death. While her game plan was all well and good in theory, she found herself confronted with a practical issue: the second key was no longer there. Vincent had removed the key to the bedroom door that opened onto the corridor. She was trapped – unless there was a second key in this room that fit the lock.

Systematically, Aline set out to check drawers, boxes and pockets – the usual places where people kept keys. It was a cumbersome task, as the room's inhabitant appeared to be a thoroughly disorganized person. Aline had to sift through large loose-leaf collections carelessly stashed away in desk drawers. Various personal items she came across in the process left no doubt as to the owner of the room. This was Vincent's master bedroom, and she had been locked in his en-suite bathroom. The implication was deeply worrying. Surely, none of her colleagues were so rude as to search their line manager's room as part of some team-building hide-and-seek game. She felt certain that her Super-Sector-Leader had deliberately hid her in the one place where nobody would come looking for her. And in order to prepare for every contingency, he had locked both of the doors that stood between Aline and freedom.

He must have wanted very badly to separate her from her colleagues, to lock her in his own room, she mused. Surely he would not want her to see all his personal items and documents – unless it was a moot issue because he intended to silence her before she had a chance to discuss them with anyone else. She gulped and brushed away the gloomy thought. Presumably, he had expected her to remain locked in the bathroom until he gave someone the go-ahead to liberate her. Surely, he hadn't counted on her resourcefulness to advance as far as his bedroom. Rationalizing his actions in this way calmed Aline's nerves, but she remained acutely aware that she kept evading the all-important question: *To what purpose had Vincent locked her in?* In what way could he possibly benefit from side-lining her for hours? She could not think of a single explanation that was both plausible and reassuring. Her desire to find the key to Vincent's bedroom door grew stronger than ever.

If there was a second key, it was not in Vincent's desk drawer, which she had searched inch by inch. Could it be in one of the many shoe boxes stacked in the walk-in closet? Staring at the pile of boxes, she felt overwhelmed by a sense of futility. Examining the boxes one by one was a daunting task, and she had to envisage the possibility that Vincent might walk in on her at any time. He would not be pleased to find her prying into his personal affairs; his subsequent actions might be more drastic than originally planned. And the exercise might be in vain. She had no idea whether there even was a second key stashed away somewhere in this room. She glanced at the windows once more. The storm was letting up; the wind was no longer howling. But rain kept pouring down as if it were trying to wash away Moorland Manor along with its tragic history. Leaving through the bedroom door was still a better option by far than exiting through the window.

With a sigh, Aline turned to the shoe boxes and immediately made a startling discovery. The first item she removed from the first box was a faded newspaper clipping dated November 27, 1994. It covered the tragic death of a seventeen-year-old boy named Raymond Worthington, who appeared to have slipped on a rock on Moorland Manor and fallen down the precipitous cliffs. His disappearance had been reported by the manor's other residents the next morning and his remains had soon been fished out of the sea by water police. His death was being treated as an accident.

This must be the tragedy Julia had alluded to, Aline reflected. Presumably, this Raymond Worthington was related to her line manager, Vincent Worthington. This would explain why his death had derailed Vincent. Possibly, Vincent even felt a twinge of guilt or remorse. Was it possible that he had somehow contributed to Raymond's accident? *If it was an accident,* she reflected grimly. According to the newspaper, his death *was being treated* as an accident. But could anyone ever really reconstruct the circumstances of a death that had occurred under the conditions described in the brief article? Aline was no expert in unexplained deaths, but she assumed that in case of doubt, it would be preferable to treat a death as an accident rather than a suicide, especially if the victim was a prominent citizen in that part of the world where he or she died.

Besides the newspaper clipping, the box was filled to the brim with keepsakes and old photographs. One of them showed Vincent as a young man, standing next to a fairly pretty, dark-haired young woman who held a baby boy in her arms. Vincent had never mentioned a son, but Aline remembered Julia's remark about his divorce. The lady in the picture was probably his estranged wife, and in all likelihood, she had been awarded custody of the child after the divorce. Silently, Aline emptied one box after another and checked coat pockets until she had to accept that the second key, which might or might not exist, was not hidden in the walk-in closet.

She glanced around the room indecisively, wondering what to do next. Her gaze fell on a laptop computer sitting on the small writing table next to his bed. It was her last hope. With luck, Vincent had stored a detailed agenda for this team-working off-site on the hard drive. If so, it might give her a clue as to why she had been brought to this room, how long she was to be kept in captivity and possibly even what escape routes were available to her, although she had to acknowledge that the evidence of her own eyes showed clearly that on a stormy night, there were none. She booted the computer. To her relief, it wasn't locked. She gained immediate access to every file stored on the hard drive. A quick survey provided the answer to one question she had been asking herself for months: *What did Vincent do all day in his office?* To all appearances, he spent his days thinking through every scenario imaginable for the future development of equity markets in general and his research department in particular. The Windows explorer showed nearly a dozen files that carried the words *Blue Sky* in their names. They dated back to the time when Vincent had been appointed Super-Sector-Leader.

Aline double-clicked on one of the *Blue Sky* files and gawked. In the document, Vincent had fleshed out grandiose hiring plans. The size of her own team had been expected to double, and he had planned to add many more analysts in other sectors, as well as an army of editorial staff to cope with the expected high volume of research production he expected from an enlarged department. His targets for research report output also seemed to be based on a far higher level of productivity than anyone in the department had ever displayed. The more recent files carried more somber names such as *Temporary Cutbacks* and *Crisis Management*. Aline did not bother to open any of them. Instead, she skipped to a document entitled *Last Resort*. It had been compiled only a few weeks ago and delineated the cuts that would be required if market volatility persisted. The targeted headcount reduction under the *Last Resort* scenario was staggering. Aline hoped that it included support staff; if not, the number equated to ninety percent of her department. Her initial fears were confirmed as she read on: under the *Last Resort* scenario, AgriBank would cease its pan-European stock coverage and focus exclusively on smaller stocks listed in the UK, on the grounds that the latter space was less competitive. A handful of surviving analysts would cover these names across industry sectors, thus giving up their sector specialization.

These were certainly dim prospects! Aline, who had put an inordinate amount of time and effort into understanding banking sector dynamics and regulations, wasn't sure whether she should hope that she would keep her job if the *Last Resort* scenario played out. The lure of a fat severance package might prove irresistible. At least she now held the clue to Vincent's panicky behavior and the frequent, erratic changes in direction she had observed recently. She had known instinctively that Vincent appeared to be under increasing pressure to justify the existence of his large, over-staffed, underperforming department, but she never would have guessed that her employer was mulling a quasi-exit from Equity Research. Developments appeared to have gathered pace in recent weeks and months: the *Blue Sky* ambitions and the desperate *Last Resort* measures were separated in time by less than six months. Little wonder Vincent kept trying new success formulas, ranging from joint research pieces and spamming clients' answering machines to a random reshuffle of the metrics used to gauge analysts' success, in a frantic effort to pacify AgriBanks' executives and buy time for his department.

Maybe it really was time to start mapping out her post-AgriBank life – as soon as she had returned safely to London. Unfortunately, her foray into the administrative aspects of the AgriBank research department had not brought her any closer to her immediate goal of escaping from Vincent's bedroom. She had not detected a single file relating to the off-site on Moorland Manor. She was somewhat reassured by the absence of any files entitled *Silencing Aline Alexandre*, but then it was unlikely that anyone would store such a document on a work computer.

The time had come for her to make a decision. As far as she could tell, she had two choices. She could either stay put, hoping that her captivity was nothing more than a silly joke and that sooner or later, Vincent would liberate her. Or she could escape through the window, climbing down the slippery gutter in the pouring rain. She did not relish the prospect of another climbing adventure, but if she was careful, the chance of suffering a debilitating accident on her way down was slim. Her relative assessment of risk and safety thus depended on the extent to which she could trust Vincent. Was he merely an eccentric old geezer who ultimately wouldn't harm a fly? Or was a he a deranged, sadistic killer?

In search of an answer to this all-important question, she did not have many clues to rely on. She could not discount the possibility that Vincent himself had orchestrated the strange incidents that had taken place over the weekend. He had had more opportunity to poison the food than anyone else. True, he had claimed that he had been ill as well, and he had looked ashen at the breakfast table the next morning. But since he slept in a separate location from the analysts and Aline had not seen him during that memorable night, she had only his word for it. And with his fair complexion, it was not difficult for him to look ashen. He was the one who had made Aline's group climb a tree that was exceptionally ill-suited to the purpose. He had personally made sure that Aline would be taken to a hiding place where she was unlikely to be found by her colleagues. Since he controlled the activity schedule, he was more likely than any of the analysts to be able to sneak into Aline's room unseen to place a dead mouse by her bedside. And she could not exclude the possibility that he had penned the tasteless *Reality Check* note. He had had plenty of time to prepare notes before summoning everyone to the library, and it would have been easy to slip it into the bag unnoticed.

If he had written the note, it implied that he was not in possession of his full faculties. Whatever he thought of Aline as an employee, she was not in a position to do anything which her line manager could construe as *playing cat and mouse* with him. What if he *was* a lunatic? She had never contemplated the possibility before, but she had to recognize that all the pieces of the puzzle fit this new theory beautifully, including the tragic death that had occurred in his family more than fifteen years ago, and which still haunted him to the point where he held on to newspaper clippings on the subject. The thought of Raymond Worthington's regrettable *accident* cinched it. She decided in favor of an escape through the window.

8 LIBERATION

It proved to be a difficult but manageable task. The hardest part was reaching the gutter in the first place. Working her way along the horizontal portion to reach the vertical part was a slippery affair. But once she had attained the vertical section, gliding down was easy. Inevitably, Aline was soaked by the time she reached the ground. The dark sky and pouring rain made it difficult for her to see clearly, as she looked around uncertainly, trying to decide on a course of action. She realized that she was dangerously close to the edge of the cliff, and the ambiance below bore no resemblance to the peaceful scenery she had contemplated in the morning. The sandy beach was no longer visible. Tall waves were smashing furiously against the rocks, their white crests hissing, as if they were seeking vengeance against Moorland Manor for some monstrous past injustice.

All of a sudden, Aline noticed that she was not alone. Close to her left ear, a familiar voice said: "There you are"."

She whirled around and stood face to face with Vincent. Incredibly, he had searched for her outside despite the raging storm. He must have gone to some trouble to look for her; his clothes were nearly as wet as Aline's.

"Here I am", Aline chirped, trying to sound light-hearted. There was still an infinitesimal chance that she would be able to trick him into believing that she mistook the dire events that had taken place at Moorland Manor over the weekend for fun and games. It was her only chance. Presently, she realized that her hope was forlorn.

"This is the exact same spot where my son Raymond killed himself", Vincent murmured in a toneless voice, looking across the wild sea. Aline's heart began to pound. Was this just an off-topic remark, a painful memory which this secluded spot had brought back to him? Or was he concerned that she intended to jump? Would he push her if necessary? She knew that she could not possibly survive a fall down the cliff into the agitated sea. The waves would smash her against a rock, and then she would lose consciousness and drown. She also realized that her death would be treated as an accident; it was easy enough to slip on the wet grass and stones in a violent storm. She darted a quick glance at Vincent's limbs. He did not look strong, but then Aline was exceptionally small. She had always been a fighter, but it dawned on her that most of her battles had been wars of words. She tried to remember the last time she had prevailed in a physical fight and could not recall a single instance beyond her kindergarten years when she had resorted to using fists. Would she be able to fend off a possible attack by Vincent? Involuntarily, she felt her muscles twitch as she prayed that she would not have to pit her seven-and-a-half stone frame against this crazy and possibly desperate old man. She soon realized that she was safe for the time being, as Vincent's mind was on events that had taken place in a distant past.

"He was like you", he reminisced, shaking his head sadly. "He was too successful."

Too successful? Vincent's words reverberated in Aline's mind. She was still reeling from his *You'll never be good enough* speech the previous day. How on earth had she gone from being a complete failure to being too successful in the space of twenty-four short hours? Aline thought that she ought to feel either fear or anger. Instead, a horrible wave of pity for this pathetic little shriveled-up man, mixed with disgust, came over her.

Vincent took another step towards Aline. "Why are you so unhappy?" he inquired. The pain in his voice struck a note of sincerity.

Aline stared at him incredulously. "I am not unhappy!" she snapped. "In fact, I am very happy whenever I'm not being locked up in dark rooms by some lunatic!" She never knew what prompted her to add "But if I'd had a father like you, I would have jumped, too!"

She bit her lips, wishing she could swallow her words. She registered an expression of shock and indescribable pain on Vincent's face. All was lost now, she thought, panic-stricken. Vincent would fly into a fury and push her over the cliff. She braced herself, but to her amazement, he simply continued to stare at her with a forlorn look on his face. This was not the face of a murderer about to tackle his victim, she thought. Instead, he looked as if he were about to burst into tears.

"I was only trying to help you!" he cried in despair. His tone might have been used by a three year-old who found himself unexpectedly scolded by his mother.

"Help me?!?" Aline echoed in disbelief. *If anyone needed help, it was Vincent,* she thought.

"You see, you are one of our best analysts. But you are too independent, too sure of yourself. You think you don't need your colleagues because you are successful. But it's easy to be successful when you don't have a strong team. And as your manager, I can't condone your behavior just because you are successful. After all, Edward's problem was that he was too successful. I am just trying to help you to learn to trust your colleagues and build a career."

Aline was lost for words. So he had locked her in and subjected her to all this agony, for the sole purpose of letting her stew for a while before driving home the message that teamwork was important? Never mind that his speech was not even beginning to make sense. Edward had worked for a department that was not even remotely connected to Equity Research. His 'problem' had been that he had defrauded AgriBank to the tune of hundreds of millions of pound sterling and had been found out eventually. There were no successes he could claim for himself, other than the fact that his unlawful activities had gone unnoticed for extended periods of time owing to the bank's inadequate risk management and fraud detection systems. Vincent's assertions that it was easier for an individual to succeed than it was for a team was simply counterintuitive; and if management trusted their own logic, the expense of hiring teams was unjustifiable from the point of view of the bank's shareholders. She had long suspected Vincent of opportunistically regurgitating the opinions of whatever individuals he had spoken to most recently, without thinking things through. But surely he could not fail to notice the contradictions in his recent admonitions! Her doubts with respect to Vincent's sanity were stronger than ever, as she stared back at him in horror.

"But it's cold and wet here", Vincent continued calmly. "Let's schedule a meeting to discuss when we're back in the office."

"My next meeting will be with HR!" Aline, who had found her speech again, shouted indignantly.

"You're going to complain to HR?" Vincent asked incredulously, as if he could not believe that someone would rat on him for playing a silly but perfectly harmless prank.

"No. I'm going to resign to HR. I'm going to complain to the police. Whatever lessons you felt you had to teach me, you had no right to lock me away and to kill an innocent little mouse and to…"

"Kill a mouse?" Vincent repeated, bewildered. It was obvious that he had tagged her as stark raving mad. When he had found her by the edge of the cliff, her eyes fastened on the crashing waves below, he had misinterpreted her actions as a suicide attempt. Now, she was inventing stories about murdered mice. He thought her behavior erratic at best. "What are you talking about?"

Aline began to feel physically ill. She had been positive that the dead mouse she had found by her bedside in the morning had formed an integral part of Vincent's dubious pedagogical techniques. Now, she could sense that he was flabbergasted. But if he had not put the mouse in Aline's room, then who had? And to what end? Was there another sociopath among the AgriBank Research staff, a cat among the pigeons more dangerous than Vincent? Aline felt a more pressing need than ever to unravel the mystery. She would have to look over her shoulder until all the pieces fit together. Conversely, Vincent appeared to be unfazed by and thoroughly disinterested in the mystery of the murdered mouse and decided to drop the subject.

"It's getting late, let's go in", he observed nonchalantly and let Aline lead the way, walking close behind her and holding an arm over her shoulder as if to protect her or to strike, should the need arise.

Several hours later, Aline lay in bed, battling fatigue that seemed to envelope her and threatened to carry her off to the land of dreams. She had vowed to herself that she would not close her eyes until she had identified the mouse killer in her mind, and she would stick to her resolution at all costs. She knew that she would be unable to feel safe again until she had elucidated the prankster's motives and thus answered the all-important question: *Was he satisfied with his crude act of vengeance, or was the mouse episode just a prelude to something more frightening?*

She would start by eliminating suspects. Vincent was out of it, she decided. His astonishment at her mention of a dead mouse had been genuine. While Aline was pleased with her observation, it was only modestly reassuring. Vincent's innocence with respect to any acts of cruelty to animals did not automatically make him an emotionally well-integrated individual. Her initial relief at her escape from the locked bathroom had given rise to quiet nagging doubts. She had never heard of a line manager disciplining his charges by means of imprisonment. The more she thought about it, the more she became convinced that Vincent suffered from a personality disorder that rendered his actions inscrutable and unpredictable.

Fred could not be ruled out as a mouse murder suspect, but Aline considered him to be an unlikely candidate. Cunning and subtlety were not among his primary character traits. If he disapproved of anything Aline had said or done, he was far more likely to accost her colleagues at the coffee machine to air his grievances.

The same logic applied to Amanda. Subtlety was not within her nature; she was far more likely to pounce on something Aline said or did. She never missed an opportunity to step into the limelight, where she would voice her opinions with the appropriate dose of self-righteousness in front of an involuntary audience that pretended to listen in rapt attention. Killing mice and depositing them anonymously next to the beds of individual colleagues did not further the impression that you were more virtuous than anyone else;

and since the halo over her head was Amanda's sole concern, Aline could safely discount her as far as the mouse massacre was concerned.

Aline also determined not to waste any time on analysts who covered other sectors and rarely ever interacted with her in the course of AgriBank's business. Most of them were recent arrivals, and if any of them had an axe to grind, she would never be able to guess what it was. The same was true for Vincent's family members who currently resided on Moorland Manor. Madness might run in the family, and one of them might deliberately have left poisoned mushrooms in the pantry and placed the mouse in front of Aline's bed. However, since they didn't even know her, it would be a strange coincidence that they had placed the mouse precisely in her bedroom. Furthermore, Vincent's family was innocent as far as her adventure in the tree and the *hate mail* was concerned. However, Aline was convinced that the mystery of the murdered mouse somehow tied in with the other incidents that had occurred on Moorland Manor. Based on these deductions, she reduced the number of suspects to two. Either Tom or Julia had to be guilty.

Tom appeared to be the most plausible culprit. He was probably the author of the anonymous rant about playing cat and mouse Aline had received during the *Reality Check* session, and which had foreshadowed the gruesome find by her bedside the next morning. He was intimidated by Aline and blamed her for his shortcomings and setbacks. At the same time, he was unable to express the reasons for his rancor and to resolve conflicts openly. He had a sneaky, cruel streak and might well be fuelled by a desire to hurt Aline pointlessly. He might also be willing to sacrifice an animal in the process. But could she be sure that he had penned the *hate mail*? And if so, how confident could he have been that he would be able to catch a mouse in order to illustrate his letter with real-life events?

The more she thought about it, the more the mouse massacre seemed out of character for her passive-aggressive team-mate. Conceiving the plan to kill a mouse and to place it strategically next to your sleeping colleague without providing any clue as to the purpose or meaning of the prank required a subtler, more patient mind - a mind such as Julia's. Julia was trying hard to come across as a friendly, compassionate, perfectly normal co-worker. In fact, she was trying too hard. Nobody at AgriBank was that normal. In her semi-wakeful state, Aline harbored growing suspicions that Julia was simply trying to gain her trust for some inscrutable purpose of her own. She had to consider the possibility that Julia was the force behind all of the incidents that had occurred during the weekend. Julia had come up with the theory that inedible mushrooms had been to blame for the food poisoning that had kept them awake during their first night on Moorland Manor. Julia herself had not been ill. What if the mushrooms were a red herring, and she herself had laced the food with a toxic substance? Julia had suggested that Aline climb all the way to the tree top, an activity which had nearly resulted in a serious accident.

Julia had deliberately cast suspicion on Tom as the likely author of the *hate mail*. What if Julia was the author? Maybe she had deliberately altered her hand-writing in the anonymous letter and written a second, harmless note in her normal hand-writing to deceive Aline? Was it possible to disguise your hand-writing this successfully?

From the beginning, Julia had sought to gain Aline's trust – and had nearly succeeded. By orchestrating mysterious incidents in this secluded setting and throwing suspicion on Aline's colleagues, she might hope to get Aline into a frame of mind where she confided in the only person she perceived as a friend. But for what purpose? *If only I could find the purpose, I would hold the clue to everything,* Aline thought, and yawned. She had to think it through logically if she wanted to protect herself from another bad surprise, but she was so very tired…

Aline awoke when the door to her room opened slowly. The first rays of sunlight had found their way through her fairly loose window shutter, and Aline could see clearly the outline of a dead white mouse quivering with every step as her intruder approached softly, carefully deposited the mouse by Aline's bed, fell on its back and purred.

"That kitten must adore you!" Julia was standing in the open door, looking down at Aline's feline friend in amusement. "We had three cats at home when I was a kid and I never got any dead mice. Vincent said to tell you to hurry up. We'll get going as soon as possible in order to avoid the heavy traffic later in the day, when everyone will be returning from their bank holiday weekend."

"In other words, everyone is as desperate to leave as I am?"

"You can say that again. There's only so much team spirit anyone can take."

"Okay, tell them I'll be downstairs in ten."

9 SAFE AND SOUND

Nearly a week later, Aline was comfortably installed at a table in an Italian restaurant, with her boyfriend Jim seated across from her and a long menu of food that could be trusted implicitly in front of her.

"So there never was any real danger after all?" Jim asked casually while sipping champagne, after Aline had told her story.

"If starvation, sleep deprivation, imprisonment and near-fatal accidents don't count as danger in your book, then I suppose that, no, there never was any real danger", Aline replied, with a faint note of irritation in her voice. She had hoped for slightly more compassion after her bank holiday weekend ordeal.

"I'd be more impressed if you didn't tell me every day that your office resembles a dungeon, that they make you get up at the crack of dawn and that you don't have time to take a lunch break", Jim replied skeptically. "And you seemed to be thoroughly enjoying doing *saltos mortales* in your trapeze class."

"*Salti mortali*", Aline corrected him mechanically. Her mind was still on the events of the weekend. While she was now satisfied that the food-poisoning had been the result of human error and the dead mouse could be attributed unequivocally to the frisky black kitten, Tom's threatening note had left her feeling uneasy. Her sense of uneasiness was further increased by the fact that she still could not be quite sure that Tom was the author. The combination of a colleague who accused her of malice and swore vengeance and a line manager who was so wary of successful employees that he felt it was his duty to lock them away did not bode well for her future at AgriBank. Fortunately, her time at that outfit would soon be coming to an end.

"So how did it go with HR?", Jim wanted to know, as if he had read her thoughts.

"With HR?"

"Yes, didn't you tell Vincent you were going to resign?"

"Oh, I won't have to resign after all".

"They're firing you because you didn't co-operate in all of the off-site activities?!?" Jim asked incredulously.

"Oh, I totally forgot to tell you. Rumor has it that they're going to shut our department. Seems we're deep in the red and no amount of teamwork is ever going to get us into the black again. So there will be a voluntary redundancy program opening soon."

"I'm not surprised, to be honest. From what you said, it didn't sound like they had the foggiest what they were doing. So what are you going to do next?"

"I'm going job-hunting together with Julia. We'll have a kick-off meeting over lunch tomorrow where we'll draw up a list of all the potential employers and all the head-hunters we know and then we divide up the work. She already has a head-start because she got her feelers out as soon as she clashed with Vincent after his demotion to *Super-Sector-Leader* and she's promised to put me in touch with…. What are you grinning at?"

"Looks like your team-working seminar has yielded results after all", Jim quipped. "I don't think you were working together that well with any of your colleagues before that off-site".

Aline had to admit that there was a certain humor to the situation. Despite herself, she had to laugh.

"Julia is the only one I'm friends with. All of the others are still the same silent, huddled creatures. I still haven't a clue what's wrong with them. I think they're just intimidated by the suffocating atmosphere in the office."

"And how is Vincent, by the way?"

"Still the same" Aline shrugged. "He was just born to be miserable, I guess. They're a melancholy old family – seems Vincent's grandfather also killed himself and one of his brothers is being treated for bipolar disorder. His son's suicide and his divorce in the aftermath probably robbed him of what little character he possessed to begin with, and all the disagreements over strategy in AgriBank's boardroom didn't help. When his boss told him to get his act together without providing any specifics as to what exactly that meant, Vincent panicked, because his job had been the only thing in his life that he had managed to hang on to. That's why he pursued change for change's sake and devised all these pointless stratagems like team-working off-sites and joint research pieces."

"How on earth did you find out all that information?"

"Julia again", Aline grinned. "Don't ask me how she's always in the know. Whether one of our clients is in disarray, AgriBank is losing money or a competitor has fired an analyst, she's always in the loop."

"You haven't asked me about my updates yet", Jim said after a while.

"That's because I'm a self-centered, rugged individualist, who tends to get seriously distracted every time her life hangs in the balance."

"Please, Aline, not again", Jim retorted, rolling his eyes.

"Okay, so then tell me your news".

"Do you remember Greenfield Partners, the firm that approached me through a head-hunter a couple months ago?"

Aline nodded. Jim had been very excited about the position and his interviews had progressed well initially, before things had gone quiet on Greenfield's end.

"They've had a hiring freeze, but it's come off now. They've made me a verbal offer and I should get the paperwork in about a week's time".

"Wow, congratulations!" Aline said, suddenly feeling very animated. "So it looks like we're going to be on garden leave at the same time?"

"Yeah, we really should treat ourselves to a romantic getaway. I wonder where is the best place to go in the fall without having to take a long-haul flight".

"Why don't we go down to Cornwall?" Aline suggested.

"You're not serious!" Jim gawked.

"But I am. The scenery is spectacular and I haven't really been able to explore it during that off-site. And you said you relished the thought of spending a romantic weekend at a haunted castle."

"Do you think Vincent's family residence is for rent, though?"

"I have no idea. But surely there must be a nice little hotel tucked away somewhere, where you needn't worry about finding dead mice next to your bed, or poisoned mushrooms on your dinner plate".

"I'm sold", said Jim, smiling. "And now I don't want you to tell me ever again that your off-site wasn't worth it!"

THE END

ABOUT THE AUTHOR

Marietta Miemietz was born in Germany and has spent fifteen years working in the financial services industry in the US, Germany and the UK, mainly as a pharmaceutical equity research analyst. She decided to become an author at age five and never goes anywhere without a notebook. *Off-site* is her first book.

12147105R00032

Made in the USA
Charleston, SC
15 April 2012